THE
FIRST BOOK OF
MAGIC

EDWARD STODDARD first learned magic from an uncle who was a minister and used it in his work with children. Mr. Stoddard has invented and sold many tricks to professional magicians and enjoys doing hypnotism and giving mind-reading demonstrations. Mr. Stoddard was born in China of missionary parents and has lived in California, Illinois, Wyoming, Kentucky, Georgia, Wisconsin, Arkansas, Indiana, and New York. By profession he is a bookseller and author, and his major hobbies (after magic) are sailing and maritime history.

THE FIRST BOOK OF MAGIC

EDWARD STODDARD

Illustrated by Rod Slater

AN AVON CAMELOT BOOK

AVON BOOKS
A division of
The Hearst Corporation
105 Madison Avenue
New York, New York 10016

CONTENTS

Magic is fun. It's fun to do and fun to watch—if it fools people.

The First Secret

It's not really tricks that fool people. It's the person who does the tricks. That is the first secret of magic.

Magicians know how to make a person look somewhere else when they have to do something they want to hide. You see, it's hard to fool a person's eyes. A magician's hand is not really quicker than the eye. But nobody can see two things at once. If you know how to make people look at one hand, they won't see what you are doing with the other hand.

In this book you will find dozens of easy tricks with money, string, handkerchiefs, balls, cards, and other things. They have all fooled people over and over. But they will fool your friends only if *you* do them the right way.

The Second Secret

The second secret of magic is that most of the time you don't really fool people's eyes. You fool their brains. You make them think you did something you really didn't do at all. Or you make them forget— or never notice at all—something you really did have to do to make the trick work.

[1]

Both secrets are called "misdirection." You make your friends look where you want them to look. You make them think what you want them to think. That is what fools people. Not tricks—magicians.

So when you are learning a trick and are told to do or say something that might not seem important, do it anyway. Do it just the way you are told. There's a good reason. It's to make your trick fool people.

All the tricks in this book are easy. They've been chosen because they don't need any special equipment from a magic store. You'll find almost everything you need in your home. For two or three of the tricks, you'll need to go to the five-and-ten for some supplies. Later, you may want to buy some magic equipment. There's a magic store in or near almost every town.

Now here are some tips on how to be a good magician.

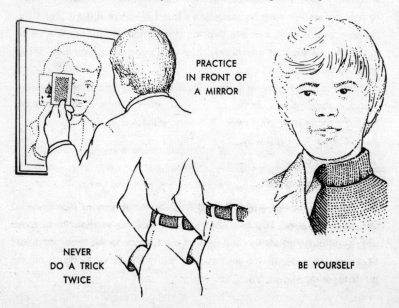

PRACTICE IN FRONT OF A MIRROR

NEVER DO A TRICK TWICE

BE YOURSELF

Six Rules for
Good Magicians

1. Practice each trick many times before you show it to anyone. If you try showing it before you've really learned it, you'll just give it away or have it fail.

2. Never, never tell your friends how you did a trick—no matter how much they beg. As soon as they find out, all the mystery is gone. They won't even be excited about other tricks you do, once they find out how simple the secrets really are. Don't be rude—just say, "I promised never to tell."

3. Never do the same trick again right away. The first time you do it, your friends don't know what will happen next. If you do it again, they know what is going to happen and will watch every move. So they see things they didn't see the first time—things you don't want them to see! Do another trick instead.

4. Don't boast. This just makes your friends angry. Even if you fool them, they won't want to see another trick. It's no fun knowing magic if people don't want to watch. So act as if you are as surprised as they are.

5. Be yourself when you do your tricks. Don't try to change your personality. You can be clownish or serious, calm or excited, slow-moving or fast-moving—whatever you naturally are. There are many different styles of presenting every trick. Be yourself.

6. Choose the tricks you like best. No person on earth could do every single trick in this book equally well. As you try them, some will feel "right" for you and others won't. Stick to the ones that feel right. You will do them best.

Now go ahead. You'll have fun!

TRICKS WITH HANDKERCHIEFS

The Knot That Ties Itself

Imagine being able to take a handkerchief out of your pocket, shake it a few times, and have a real knot tie itself in the corner!

The secret is that you already have a loose knot tied in one corner. Don't pull it tight—then someone could tell that it didn't really tie itself. Have the handkerchief in your pocket with the knot on top, where you can feel it when you reach in your pocket.

"Did you ever see a knot tie itself?" you ask your friends. When they say they haven't ask to borrow a handkerchief. But before anyone offers you one, put *both* hands in your pockets. "Never mind," you say. "Here's one."

All this makes them think that any handkerchief will do. They won't suspect that anything has been done to yours.

Hold the knot in your hand as you bring out your handkerchief. Let the rest of it hang straight down. With your other hand, take the lowest corner and bring it up so you can hold it with the first two fingers of the same hand that is hiding the knot.

Shake your hand up and down, letting go the plain corner with your fingers so it flips down. Raise your hand and look at the hanging corner. No knot.

Do It Twice

"It takes a couple of tries," you say as you do it once again. Again, no knot.

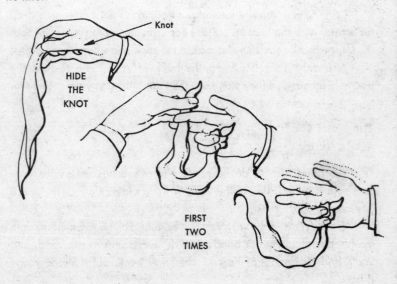

Knot

HIDE
THE
KNOT

FIRST
TWO
TIMES

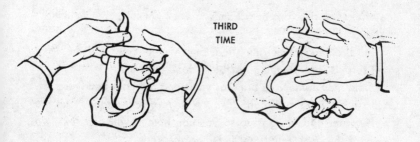

THIRD
TIME

Take the hanging corner in your fingers again, and jerk it just the way you did before. This time, let go the knot and hold on to the plain corner between your fingers. The hidden corner flips down. Now there is a knot!

Give the handkerchief to your friends. They can't find anything wrong.

Don't forget to try *twice* without getting a knot before you drop the corner with the knot in it. This keeps anyone from suspecting that the knot was already there. It makes the trick seem harder, too.

And don't forget to keep the back of your hand toward the people watching, so they won't see the knot before you want them to.

The Knot That Melts Away

This is a good trick to do next. After someone has untied the knot and says it is real, tie another one in the middle. Blow on it, and it just melts away!

The secret is in the way you tie the knot. Follow the pictures with the handkerchief in your hands, and do everything as you read, and you'll find it's easy. Any handkerchief will work, but a slippery one is best.

Take one end of the handkerchief between the first and second fingers of your left hand. See picture A. Now, with your right hand, carry the other end up between your left second and third fingers. Hold it between your left thumb and first finger. It should look like picture B.

Now, with your right hand, reach *through* the loop that hangs down (picture C). Take the end you are holding between your first and second fingers (end X). Pull that end back through the loop. Be sure to keep tight hold with your left second and third fingers. If you let these go, the knot will fall apart before you want it to.

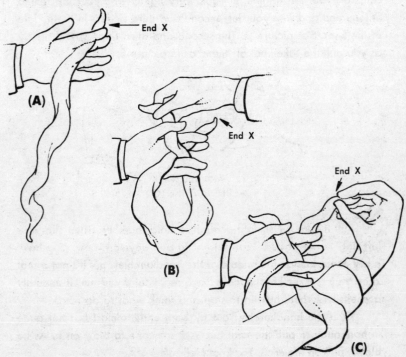

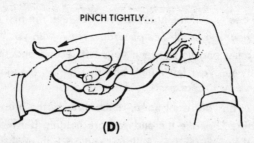

PINCH TIGHTLY...

(D)

Pull the Knot

Pull the end in your right hand toward you. Let the knot tighten and come off your left fingers. But hold very tightly with your left thumb on one end and with your left second and third fingers in the middle of the knot. See picture D. The second and third fingers hold tightly as you pull the fake knot off them, as in picture E.

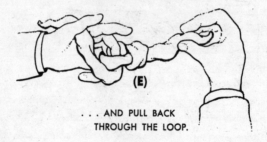

(E)

. . . AND PULL BACK
THROUGH THE LOOP.

Pull the knot just tight enough to hold together. Then slip your left fingers out of it. Be careful not to pull anymore now. You have a big, loose knot in the middle of the handkerchief, but it's not a real knot. It's just a slip knot. It looks like a real knot if you "tie" it smoothly and easily *without* having to stop and think what to do next.

Hold the handkerchief out by both ends, almost but not quite tight enough to pull the knot out. Ask someone to blow on it. As he blows, pull on the ends. The knot melts!

The Vanishing Handkerchief

The easiest way to make a handkerchief disappear is to use what magicians call a "pull." You can buy one at any magic store. But you can easily make your own. Here is how to make your own.

Take a cardboard mailing tube about an inch wide, or a toilet paper roll. Cut off a piece about two inches long. Punch a little hole in each side near one end and bend a paper clip so one end goes through each hole. Now loop rubber bands together until you have a chain about a foot long. One end is looped to the paper clip. Pin the other end to the back of your shirt near your collar and try it on. The pull should hang a little above your belt. Add or take away rubber bands until it does.

Tuck the pull into your right hip pocket. Jam it into a corner so it stays there. Keep a small handkerchief in your left hip pocket. Wear a jacket.

Don't tell anyone that you are going to make something disappear. Let it be a surprise! Say you need a handkerchief for this trick. Reach into your right hip pocket. Close your fist around the pull and take it out of your pocket. *At the same time,* look toward your left pocket and take the handkerchief from it in your left hand.

[9]

Don't look at your right hand. Everybody will think you just found your right pocket empty.

Hold your right hand closed around the pull about an inch above and in front of your belt buckle. Tuck the handkerchief carefully into your "hand." (It really goes into the pull.)

Now Look Up

As you push the last of the handkerchief in, look up suddenly. "Did I do this trick for you before?" you ask.

The people watching say, "No." But as they say it, they can't help looking up into your eyes. The minute they look up, let go the pull. It flies back under your jacket. Keep your right hand curled up as if the handkerchief were still there.

"Then I'll show you how to make a handkerchief disappear," you say. Slowly raise your right fist and point to it with your left hand. Let them see your left hand is empty.

Snap your left fingers and at the same time open your right hand. It's empty!

The secret is not to let them know that the handkerchief has disappeared until *after* it is gone.

EYES *UP*
LET PULL GO

Cutting through
Your Neck

You tie a piece of string into a loop, put it around your neck, and—zip!—pull it right through!

This is one of the few tricks in which something does happen faster than people can see. But it's easy to do.

Take a string about three and a half feet long. Tie the ends together so you have a circle. Be sure the knot is a good square knot that won't come undone.

Now pass this loop around the back of your neck and hold one end in each hand. Hold the ends by putting your first fingers inside the ends of the loop, as in picture A. Bring your hands together so the two ends of the loop are almost touching. Turn your hands so their backs are toward the people watching. This hides the ends of the loop and your fingers.

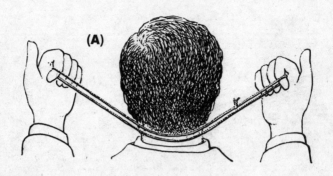

(A)

Tell everyone you can make one solid object pass through another—the string through your neck. While you are talking, slip the *second* finger of your right hand inside the same end of the loop you are holding with your left first finger. See picture B. Pull your right first finger out so that it barely holds its end of the loop, and it can let the string go quickly and easily.

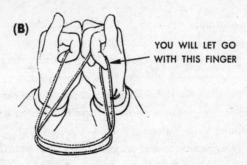

(B)

YOU WILL LET GO
WITH THIS FINGER

Wait for Attention

Wait a moment without saying anything so everyone will be watching. Suddenly say, "Now!" and spread your hands wide apart with a snap. The string will seem to melt right through your neck.

[12]

PULL YOUR HANDS
APART WITH A SNAP

What you really did was to let go the right-hand side of the loop altogether. Your left first finger and right second finger were both in the left-hand side of the loop as you snapped your hands apart. This drags the right end around your neck. It happens so fast, it actually looks as if the string cut right through you!

Practice this slowly a few times so you can see what happens. Then learn to do it with a snap.

You can use this same method to make the loop pass "through" someone else's neck, the arm of a chair, a broomstick, or anything else you want.

The Mended String

This is one of the most famous tricks in the world. Stage magicians use rope. Magicians who work close to their audience—as you do—use string.

There are dozens of ways of doing the trick. One of the newest, easiest, and best ways is this one.

Take a string three feet long. Measure it. Then, beginning six inches from one end, coil up one *third* of it neatly. The string should be two feet long now, and the coil should not be more than an inch long when flattened out. Tie a very light thread just once around its

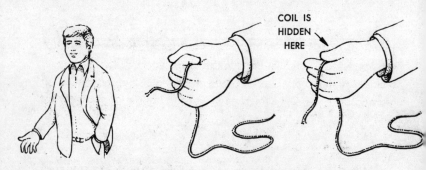

COIL IS HIDDEN HERE

middle. It should be a thread you can break easily. (Nylon thread, for example, is too hard to break.)

Put the string in your left pocket with the coil on top. Keep a pair of scissors handy. Bring out the string with your left hand, hiding the coil inside your fist. If it is tangled, straighten it out so that the short end sticks out above your fist and the long end hangs below.

Hold the short end between your left thumb and the first finger. Open your fist. Be sure to keep your fingers together and curled a little to hide the coil. Make sure nobody stands behind you or far enough to one side to see it.

Cut the String

Ask somebody to cut the string exactly in the center. Hold your left hand up high and hold the bottom end with your right hand. After the string has been cut, raise your right hand with its half hanging down. Show that the string is in two pieces.

Now take one end of the piece in your right hand and twist it with the short end sticking above your left fist. Don't tie a real knot. Then put the rest of that string into the top of your left fist. Keep your fist closed so that it bunches up tightly. Push the end of it down out of sight and poke the piece hanging out of the bottom of your left fist inside too.

Hold out your left fist with both pieces of string in it. Ask someone to blow on it.

With your right hand, take the end of the string from the *bottom* of your fist and begin pulling. Pull slowly. When the string is half out, begin watching it instead of your hand. Lower your left hand a little and let your right hand start to rise. Watch the middle of the string.

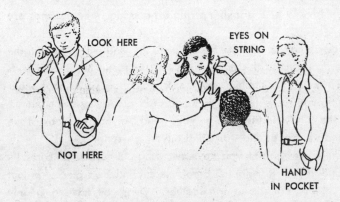

LOOK HERE

NOT HERE

EYES ON STRING

HAND IN POCKET

Keep your left fist closed tight. When the string reaches the coil, the thread will break and the coil will unwind.

By the time you reach the end of the string, your right hand should be high and your left hand should be almost as low as your waist. Don't look at your left hand. Let it drop slowly while you hold your right hand up high and look closely at the middle of the string. Hold it toward someone and ask him to see if he can find the cut.

As everyone looks at the string, slowly and easily put your left hand in your pocket and leave the extra piece of string. Just as slowly and naturally take your hand out and let it hang by your side. Don't look at it at all.

If you do this as you ask someone to watch the string, and look at the string yourself, nobody will notice or remember that you had your hand in your pocket.

The string is perfectly mended. It's the same length it was at first!

The Ring through the String

Another famous trick is taking a ring off a string while the ends are held.

For a ring, use a white candy mint—the kind with a hole in the middle. You thread this on a string and someone holds both ends tight. Throw a handkerchief over the string. Putting your hands under the cloth, you say a few magic words. You pull away the handkerchief. The candy ring is lying on your hand. Anyone can look at the mint and the string, and won't find anything wrong!

The secret is that you have *two* rings. Beforehand, carefully snap one in two. If it doesn't break cleanly into two pieces without loose crumbs, eat it and try another. When you have a cleanly broken one, wet the broken edges and hold the pieces together until they dry. If the crack shows, rub some powdered sugar over it.

Put this broken and mended candy mint back in the pack. Have a handkerchief in your pocket with another unbroken mint.

Borrow the string if you can, but be sure to have one in case you can't borrow any. Take out the pack of candy, pry the broken mint off the top, and thread the string through it. Ask two different

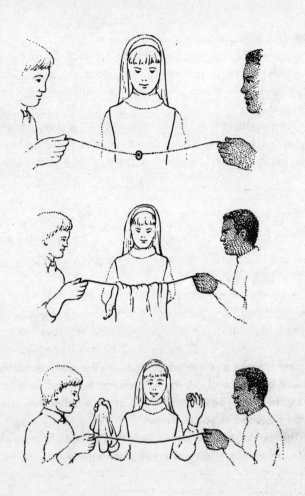

people to hold the ends of the string. Reach into your pocket and put the extra candy ring in your hand. Bring out the handkerchief in the same hand. Spread the handkerchief over the mint on the string. Keep your hand closed around the extra candy.

Break the Mint

Reach under the handkerchief with both hands. Snap the already broken mint in two. Be sure not to drop one of the pieces. Close your hand around them. Open your other hand with the whole mint ring on the palm.

Say something like "Abracadabra" or "Om mani padme hum." Bring out the hand that has the broken mint and use that hand to lift off the handkerchief. Stuff the handkerchief into your pocket while

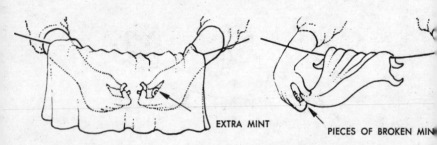

EXTRA MINT

PIECES OF BROKEN MIN

everyone is looking at the whole mint in your other hand. Push the pieces of broken candy down past the handkerchief deep into your pocket. Then if anyone wants to look at the handkerchief, you won't spill the pieces when you pull it out.

The reason you break the candy mint ahead of time is so that it won't crack noisily when you break it during the trick.

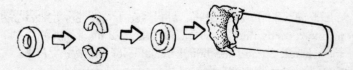

The Invisible Dime

Some of the very best tricks in magic are so simple you can hardly believe they will fool anyone.

This is one of those tricks. It is bold. It will work only if you do it exactly right. But if you do it right, it is a real stunner.

What you seem to do is take a dime in one hand and, while your friend holds your wrist, make it disappear. As simple as that.

But the secret is all in the acting. Because the dime was never in your hand to begin with!

How to Get Ready

You get ready for this trick by making sure you have one dime, a nickel, and three quarters in a pocket. If you have more change than that with you, keep it in another pocket. You want to pull out the dime, nickel, and three quarters all together when you are ready to do the trick.

Start by saying, "I just learned a nifty new trick with a dime. May I show you?"

Do *not* say anything about making the dime disappear. In almost all tricks, it is important not to say ahead of time what you are going to do.

When your friend says sure, pull out all the change in your right hand. Jingle it around on your palm. "I think I have a dime here," you say. Jingle the change around until the dime is on your palm near one of the quarters.

Now do this with every bit of acting you can manage. Reach down with your left fingers as if you are going to pick up the dime. As soon as your left fingers are over it, just slide the dime under the

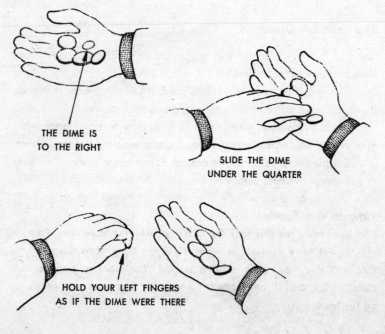

THE DIME IS
TO THE RIGHT

SLIDE THE DIME
UNDER THE QUARTER

HOLD YOUR LEFT FINGERS
AS IF THE DIME WERE THERE

quarter. Hold the left fingers as if the dime were there and lift your left hand up to shoulder level.

Look at your left hand. Forget your right hand. *Think* that the dime is in your left hand. Try to believe that it really is there.

The Secret Is Acting

That is really the whole secret. If you act it out right, your friend will swear later that he saw the dime in your left hand. Honest. It works.

Dump the rest of the change back in your pocket. The dime is safely out of the way. Close your left hand into a fist. Have your friend hold your wrist to make sure you don't hide the dime in your sleeve.

"Now," you say, "I'm going to make the dime disappear."

Use any magic words you like, or make mysterious passes with your right hand over your left fist. "Going . . . going . . . gone!"

Open your left hand. Of course the dime is gone!

This trick will fool people if you do it just the way you are supposed to. If you feel guilty about the change in your right hand, or act suspiciously when you pretend to pick up the dime, it may not work. It's all in the acting.

Rubbing a Quarter Away

All you need for this trick is a quarter. It should be your own quarter, because after you make it disappear you can't get it back again right away.

Tell your audience you're going to rub the quarter through your elbow. Take the quarter in your right hand. Bend your left arm and rest your left hand on the back of your neck so you can see your elbow.

Rub the quarter against your elbow with your right fingers. After four or five rubs, let it slip out from under your finger and fall to the floor.

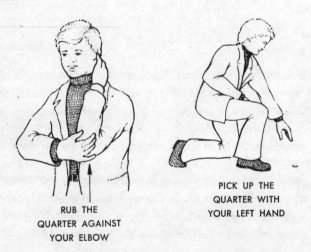

RUB THE
QUARTER AGAINST
YOUR ELBOW

PICK UP THE
QUARTER WITH
YOUR LEFT HAND

Pick up the quarter with your *left* hand. Put it in your right hand. Put your left hand behind your neck again and go on rubbing.

Drop the quarter again. Pick it up again and begin rubbing. After a moment, take your right hand away. The quarter is gone. Both your hands (and sleeves) are empty!

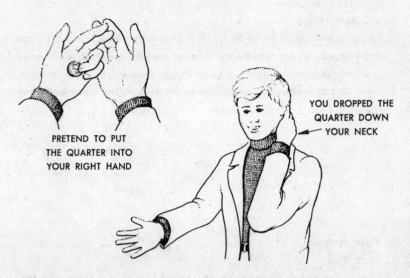

PRETEND TO PUT THE QUARTER INTO YOUR RIGHT HAND

YOU DROPPED THE QUARTER DOWN YOUR NECK

The Secret

The second time you drop the quarter, pick it up in your left hand just as you did the first time. Pretend to put it back in your right hand. But, instead, just bring your hands together and leave the quarter in the left hand. Don't pay any attention to this at all. Don't look at your left hand. Put it behind your neck again and, with your right fingers tight together, begin rubbing your elbow. Your left hand drops the quarter down your collar, and there you are!

Be sure to drop the quarter *twice*. It gets everyone used to your picking it up with your left hand and putting it in your right hand.

Penny, Nickel,
Dime, Quarter

This Trick Needs
a Secret Helper

Nobody will be able to figure out how you know what coin has been hidden under the teacup! You go out of the room while your audience decides whether it is to be a penny, nickel, dime, or quarter. Then someone turns the cup upside down over it. You come back and tell what it is.

PENNY   NICKEL   DIME   QUARTER

Your Helper
Tells You

One of the people in the room tells you which coin is under the teacup—but he doesn't have to say a word. He tells you by the way he puts the cup over the coin!

Imagine that the handle of the teacup is a pointer. The friend who is secretly helping you puts down the cup with the handle away from you if the penny is under it. If it's the nickel, he puts the handle pointing to the right. If it's the dime, the handle points toward you. And if it's the quarter, the handle points to the left.

Simple as this seems, just try it. Be sure not to look at your secret helper, and make him promise to keep from laughing. He has to act just as surprised as everyone else is.

TRICKS WITH BALLS

The Amazing
Cups and Balls

This is one of the oldest tricks in the world. It came from India many years ago, and it's as good as ever. People just can't believe their eyes when the little balls pass right through the solid cups, again and again!

You can use three paper cups and three little balls made by cutting up a rubber sponge. The paper cups should be the round kind that have a "false bottom"—when turned upside down, there is a rim around the top. If you like the trick enough, you can get sets of cups and balls in different sizes from any magic store.

The secret is that you have an extra ball. The people watching never know about this fourth ball.

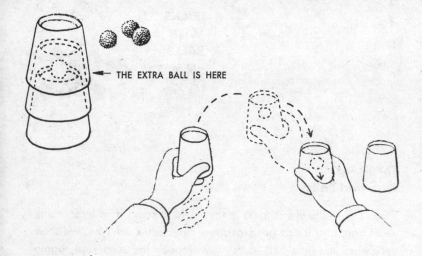

← THE EXTRA BALL IS HERE

Step 1

When you begin, the cups are stacked upside down, each one inside the next. The extra ball is in the space between the bottom cup and the middle cup. Three balls are on the table.

Begin by picking up the three cups in your left hand, still nested together. Take the *top* one in your right hand and put it mouth down on the table.

The way you do this is important. With your left hand, move all three cups up with a little jerk and pull the top cup off almost—but not quite—at the top of the jerk. Put the top cup down quickly and smoothly. Always put the cups down just this way because sometimes they will have balls in them. You must keep the ball from falling out as you put the cup down, but still make it look as if there is nothing in the cup. So you must put it down faster than the ball can fall. The little toss of all three cups makes the ball hang in the cup for a moment before you put it down. *Always use the toss!*

Put the middle and top cups down on top of one another. Use the little toss each time. You should always put the cups down the same way whether or not they have balls in them. Practice keeping the ball inside the upside-down cup with just a hint of a toss. It's not really noticeable. Each cup goes over the one below it, so you have them nested again. As you put them down, count, "One, two, three."

When you have finished, the secret extra ball will be in the middle cup. Since they are upside down, the ball will be resting on the false bottom of the lowest cup.

Step 2

"Now watch," you say as you pick up the cups and put each one mouth down on the table again. Do it again with the little swoop up of the cups in your left hand. But this time put them in a row.

The secret ball is on the table under the middle cup.

Put one of the three other balls on the base of this cup.

"One ball here," you say.

Pick up the cup on the left and drop it mouth down over the cup with the ball on it. Drop the other cup on top.

Tap the cups with your finger. "Pass!" you order.

Pick up the three cups. The ball seems to have gone right through the cup! There it is on the table.

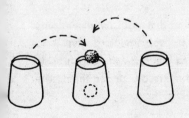

Step 3

Hold the stacked cups as before. Put them down left to right just as you did before. The *middle* cup goes over the ball that just "passed through" a cup.

The ball you put on top of the middle cup is now on the table beside the first ball. But nobody knows about this.

Pick up another ball from the table. Put it on the middle cup as you did before. Put the other cups on top. Tap them. "Pass!"

Pick up all three cups. Two balls on the table:

Now repeat step 3, doing exactly the same thing with the cups and the last ball. When you pick them up, three balls are on the table!

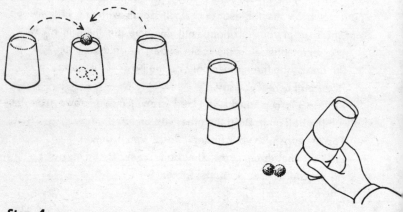

Step 4

Now you have to get rid of the extra hidden ball. Hold the cups mouth *up* in your left hand. Take out the *top* one and give it to someone to look at. While you hand it to him, turn the cups upside down in your left hand. Be sure your fingers are under them. The extra ball inside rolls out into your fingers.

GETTING RID OF
THE EXTRA BALL

Quickly curl your fingers around the ball. Pick up the cups with your right hand. As you hold them out to someone else to look at, put the extra ball in your left pocket.

Make sure to practice this until you know how to put the cups down exactly the same whether or not there is a ball inside.

The Ball That Rolls by Itself

Put a marble on a table after letting someone examine it to be sure it is ordinary. At your command, it will mysteriously roll toward you—away from you—back and forth! Anyone can pick it up without finding anything wrong.

Take a fairly large plain ring and tie two strong threads to it. Now put the ring in the center of the table and stretch each of the threads out to the edge. Tie them together under the table so they don't hang down more than three or four inches but are not too tight to move. Then lay a tablecloth on top.

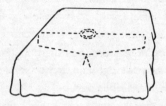

Drop the marble carefully on the cloth—within the circle of the ring. Lean over the table (you should be sitting down) with your chest close to the edge. Wave one hand over the marble while your other hand pulls the thread back and forth.

If anyone gets suspicious and wants to take off the tablecloth, just break the thread. Then pull thread and ring out from under the cloth and stuff them into your pocket.

The Wandering
Sponge Balls

The "Cups and Balls" is an old trick. The "Wandering Sponge Balls" is quite new. It's a favorite with magicians.

You will need four little balls made of sponge rubber, and one big one. Get a very soft rubber or plastic sponge from the dime store. Try to get one as close to skin color as possible. In any case, don't get a bright color that will be hard to conceal. Cut off four pieces about ¾ inch square. Trim the corners until they are roughly round and look alike.

Now trim the rest of the sponge until it is round. It should be about 3 inches across. If the sponge is very soft and you can squeeze up this big ball so it looks like two of the little balls held together, use it the way it is. If not, cut a slit in one side and cut sponge away on the inside until it is hollow and will squeeze small. It should squeeze small enough so you can easily hide it in your fist.

Have the four little balls and the big one in your right-hand pocket. Bring out all the little balls and put three on your left hand, holding the fourth one secretly in your right hand, squeezed between your first and second fingers.

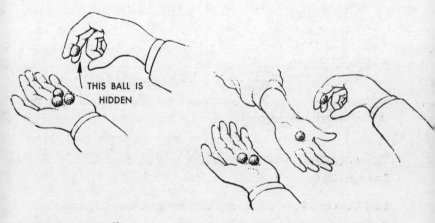

THIS BALL IS HIDDEN

The Secret Ball
If you keep your fingers together—curled in just a little—and always keep your hand *back up*, nobody will ever suspect that you have a ball in it. Especially if you remember the important rule to keep people from looking at your hand: don't look at it yourself!

With your right hand, take one of the balls from your left hand. Ask a friend to hold out her hand, palm up. Lay the ball on it. Tell her to close her fingers.

Shake your head. "Not fast enough or tight enough," you say. Take the ball back between the thumb and first finger of your right hand by putting the secret ball right on top of it and squeezing them together. At a glance, they will look like one ball.

Look her in the eye. Explain that she has to close her fist fast and hard. Give her a short look at the two balls that look like one, before you press them both into her palm. *Don't let go* until her fingers close tight.

"Now," you say, "I have two balls." Point to them. "You have one." Point to her closed fist.

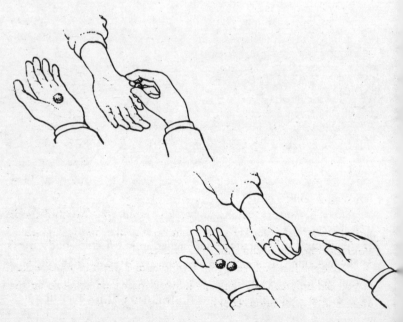

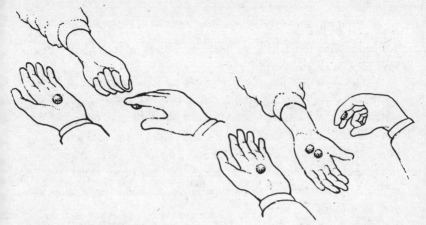

Make Her Agree

Make her agree that she has one ball.

Pick up one of the two balls from your left hand. Put your hand in your right pocket. Bring it out with the ball hidden just as you did with the extra ball before.

"One ball here." Point to your left palm. "One ball there." Point to her hand. "One in my pocket. I now command the ball in my pocket to join the one in your fist. Go!"

Tell her to open her fist. Her eyes almost pop out. Two balls!

Pick up one of the balls. "One," you count. Put it back. Pick up the other by putting the secret ball right on top and squeezing them together, just as you did before. "Two." Look her in the eye. "Now how many balls is that?"

As she answers, "Two," raise your hand. The two balls look just like one ball. Quickly push them against the one in her palm. Hold them tight until she closes her fingers.

Take the last ball from your left palm and put it in your pocket, as you did before. Only this time leave it there and squeeze up the giant ball in your hand. Look at your friend's hand.

The Last Ball Goes

"I command the last ball to go from my pocket to your hand," you say. "Go! Open your hand!"

She opens her hand and finds three balls. Right away take all three in your left hand and press them together so you can later hold them by partly closing your third and fourth fingers.

"Now you'll see some more magic," you say. Tip your left hand over your right hand, but don't let go of the three balls. With your right hand, press the giant ball quickly into her hand. Don't let go until she has closed it. Don't look at your left hand. Let it drop to your side. Forget it.

Step back and put *both* hands in your pockets, leaving the three balls. "How many balls have you?"

"Three," she will answer.

"Alakazam! Open your hand!"

She will jump when the giant ball appears on her hand. While she is staring at it, take your hands out of your pockets.

Practice this until you can do the whole routine without stopping to think what comes next. When you really know it, try it out on people. Do it quickly, going from one part of the trick into the next without giving your friends a chance to get over their surprise. It all builds up to a great big climax with the giant ball!

BOTH HANDS IN POCKETS

TRICKS WITH CARDS

NOTE: Playing cards come in Bridge or Poker width. The narrower Bridge width is much easier to use for these tricks.

The Changing Card

Imagine your friend's surprise when a card he is holding suddenly changes into another card altogether!

Borrow a deck of cards if you can. There is usually a deck in almost every home. Hold the cards face down in your left hand as if you were about to deal. See picture A. Before you begin, lift the top card. Then, with the tip of your thumb, catch the next card and lift it up too. It looks as if you were just squaring the deck. See picture B.

Now slip your left little finger under the two cards. Push them down on top of it. See picture C. If you keep the cards turned a little to the right, nobody can see.

"I want you to remember this card," you tell the person for whom you're going to do the trick.

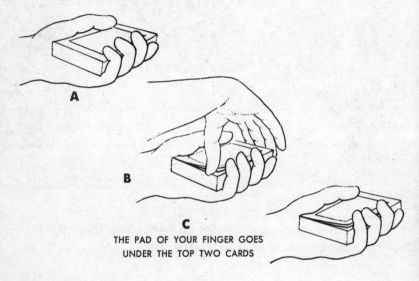

A

B

C

THE PAD OF YOUR FINGER GOES
UNDER THE TOP TWO CARDS

Reach over with your right hand. Put your right thumb at the end of the cards nearest you. Put your fingers at the other end. Lift up the two top cards as if they were one card. Hold them tightly, bent in a little, so they stay squared up. Turn your hand over and show the card. Everyone thinks it's just one card.

Make Sure
He Remembers It

Tell your friend to remember it, and make sure he does. It ruins everything if someone forgets the card.

 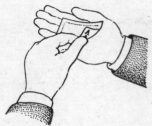

While he tells you he will remember it, put the cards back on the deck. Do this without thinking about it. Square them quickly, and deal the *top* card right away, putting it face down on his hand. Tell him to keep it there. He will think this is the card he just saw.

Ask your friend again if he remembers it. He will be a little annoyed that you don't think he can remember, so ask him to make sure and look at it again.

He will look at the card for a moment before he sees that it is a different card. Then he will nearly fall over. It seems as if the card changed while he was holding it!

You'll find that most times nobody will remember that you put the card back on the deck before giving it to your friend. It's not tricks that fool people—it's magicians!

The Telltale Face

You claim you can tell by a person's face when he is lying, and offer to prove it.

Ask someone to mix up the cards and put them face down on

the table. Reach over and cut, taking off the top half. Ask your friend to look secretly at the next card and *remember* it. Drop the top part back on the deck on top of the card he looked at. Have him cut a few times.

Now ask him to deal the cards one at a time, and turn each one face up as he deals it. He is to tell you at each card whether or not it is his. Ask him to try to fool you. You can tell when he is lying because you know when he reaches the right one!

The secret is very easy. When you take off the top part of the deck, you turn it up a little. When he is looking at his card, *you* look at the bottom card of the portion you are holding. Be sure to remember it.

No matter how often he cuts the deck, his card will be the one he deals next after the card you remember!

Behind Your Back

Every magician should know at least one trick where a friend takes a card—"any card"—and then hides it in the deck. Somehow the magician finds it again!

This way of doing the trick is very easy, but you must do it carefully. The end is a big surprise and very mysterious, because your friend's card is found *upside down* in the middle of the deck!

You do not have to get ready for this trick, except to make sure that you have a deck of cards with a white border around the back. It is much harder to do with a deck where the back design comes clear to the edge.

Here is how you do the trick.

Ask your friend to shuffle the deck as much as she wants. Take it back from her and ask her to take out one card. Let her change her mind if she wants. It does not matter what card she takes.

"Don't look at it yet," you say. "I'll turn my back while you look at it and show it to the others. Please make sure to remember it. It ruins the trick if you forget what your card was."

What You Do

Turn your back while she looks at her card. While your back is to her, turn the *whole* deck over. Now turn over just the top card. The deck looks as if it were face down because of the top card. This is why you should use a deck with white borders on the back, so nobody can see the difference from the edges.

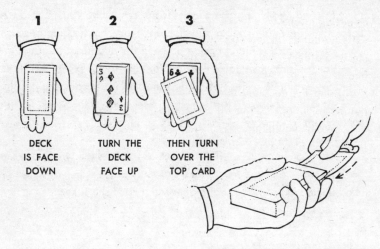

1

DECK
IS FACE
DOWN

2

TURN THE
DECK
FACE UP

3

THEN TURN
OVER THE
TOP CARD

THE DECK *SEEMS* TO BE FACE DOWN

"Are you ready?" you ask. Turn around and hold the deck while she slides her card anywhere she wants in the middle. Let her change her mind if she wants, and slide it in higher or lower, until she is satisfied. Just don't let her take the deck or open it at all. Otherwise she might see that the deck is face up under the top card.

Once your friend has decided that the card is really lost in the middle of the deck, square it up with both hands. Push all the edges of the deck to make it even, so she really knows her card is not sticking out anywhere. Show her how neat everything is.

"Now," you say, "there's no way I can tell where your card is, right?"

She has to agree.

"Just to make it even harder," you say, "I'll try to find it behind my back."

You Can't Find It

Put your hands behind your back. Turn the top card over. Then turn the whole deck over. Look puzzled. "That's funny. I can't seem to find it."

Bring the deck out from behind your back. "Are you sure you put the card back?" Your friend reminds you that you saw her do it.

"Well," you might say, "Let's look at the faces." Turn the deck face up. Begin going through the cards.

Suddenly you find one card face down in the middle of the face-up cards. Look surprised. "How do you suppose that got in here? What was your card, anyway?"

Your friend names her card. Turn over the mysterious face-down card. It's hers! And she can look over the deck as much as she likes!

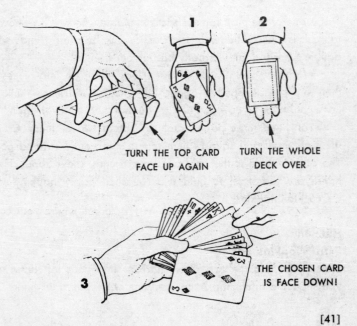

1
TURN THE TOP CARD
FACE UP AGAIN

2
TURN THE WHOLE
DECK OVER

3
THE CHOSEN CARD
IS FACE DOWN!

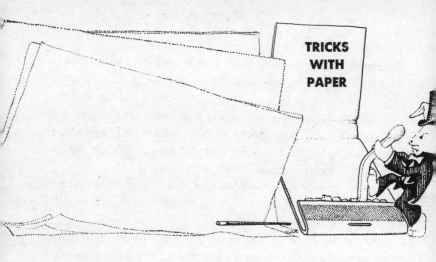

TRICKS
WITH
PAPER

The Torn Napkin

This is one of the most famous tricks in magic. The way we show you to do it is even better than the classic way, because it ends with a double surprise that will really baffle your friends.

What you seem to do is tear a paper napkin into pieces and then put it back together again. But when your friends think they have caught on to how you did it, you fool them all over again!

You need three paper napkins. Unfold two of them. Crumple them up small and squash them together in your left-hand pocket. The other napkin is the only one your friends know about. If your hands are too small to hold two squashed paper napkins easily, use cocktail napkins.

Hide the
Extra Napkins
Start by getting the two secret napkins into your left hand while you show the other napkin to everyone with your right hand. Then

open this out by taking one corner in your left hand. Keep the two squashed napkins behind the napkin they know about.

"Now," you say, "I'm going to try something that only works sometimes. Let's see if we're going to be lucky today."

Very slowly, tear the opened napkin into strips. Make sure everybody sees that you are really tearing it. Then turn the strips sideways and tear them into pieces too. "We make our own confetti," you might say.

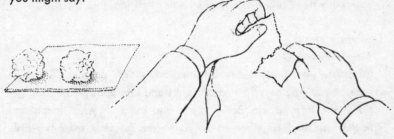

As soon as the napkin is torn into pieces, casually wad all the pieces together in your right hand. Not too tightly, though. You want this crumped napkin to look about the size of the other two in your left hand.

Finish wadding the napkin in your right hand, with your left hand, back up, pushing the pieces in. If you don't think about the two napkins in your left hand, nobody else will either. Turn your right hand palm up and look at the napkin. Take a final poke with your left first finger.

With your two hands together, look suddenly into the nearest person's eyes and say, "Did you bring your magic powder?"

Everyone will look at him. They just can't help it. At that moment, turn your left hand palm up, and your right hand palm down. Let your right hand drop slowly to your side. Forget about it.

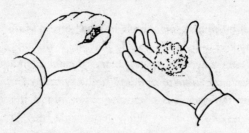

Everyone will think you just put the torn napkin in your left hand, but you really have two whole napkins squashed together there.

Finding the
Magic Powder

Of course your friend does not have any magic powder. "Maybe I have some," you say. Stick your right hand into your pocket and get rid of the torn napkin. Bring your hand out with your thumb and fingers pinched together as if you were holding some invisible powder. Sprinkle it over the napkins. Smile. Lift up the wad and carefully open one of the napkins, hiding the other one behind the one you are opening. Success!

But just as your friends are looking surprised, let the other napkin drop to the floor. Pretend not to see it. Someone is sure to

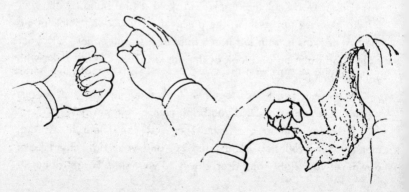

shout and point. If not, look horrified and glance down. Wait a bit. Let the suspense build.

"Oh, well," you say. "At least I have some more magic powder."

Sprinkle more "magic powder " on the napkin on the floor. Let one of your friends pick it up and open it out himself. Double surprise!

This is one trick you really must practice many times in front of a mirror before you try it out on friends. It is not hard, but you have to do it smoothly and without having to think of what to do next.

Learn it well, and it will be one of your favorites.

The Rolling Matchbook

Here is a simple little puzzle that will drive your friends wild. You can make an empty paper matchbook roll over, but they can't.

Get hold of a matchbook that has all the matches gone. Curve it like the picture, by pressing it with your fingers until it holds the shape by itself. When you are shaping it, if you curve it a bit more than the picture it will spring back to just the right shape.

Now balance it *upside down*. The folded end goes on the table. Hold it steady by keeping one finger on the end with the staple. Give the matchbook a tiny push toward the curved side and let go. It will roll clear over and do a flip-flop before it stops with the curved side up. If it does not, curve it a little more and try again. Be very sure to start with the staple end up. This is really the whole trick.

He Can't Do It

After you do a couple of flip-flops, pick up the matchbook to set the curve again. Put it back on the table with the staple end *down*. Let your friend try it. When he lets go, the matchbook just flops down and lies there rocking gently. It won't flip at all.

Let him try it a couple of times. Then pick it up, set the curve, and put it down with the staple at the top. Do a couple more flip-flops. Set the curve again and set it up for him with the staple at the bottom. Again, no flip.

Quit after this, because he might catch on if you keep doing it.

The Three Choices

This clever trick uses an old, old secret called "The Magician's Choice." Your friend thinks he makes all the choices, but always winds up choosing what you want him to!

You don't have to practice this in front of a mirror, but you do have to practice it in your head until you can go through the whole trick calmly and with a lot of confidence.

You start by talking about the mysterious way in which you can sometimes make people do what you want them to—by magic. Offer to prove it. Get three small pieces of paper. It is best to borrow them if you can, to prove that you did not get anything ready beforehand.

On one paper you print "you will choose this paper." On the other two you print "Not this one." Don't let him see which paper has which message.

Remember
Which Is Which

Crumple up the three pieces. Make very sure to remember which is the piece he is to choose. You can crumple it a little differently from the others if you want. Or crumple it first and put it at one end of the row.

Now look at the three balls of paper. Look at your friend. "I'm going to try to make you choose one piece of paper by a process of elimination. There is a message on the paper to tell you whether I did it right or not. Are you ready to try? Take your time."

Pick Up Two

When he is ready, tell him to pick up two balls. What you say next depends on whether he picks up the right ball as one of the two.

You have to be ready to give different answers without stopping to think about them. That is why you should practice before you show the trick.

If the right ball is one of the two he is holding, say right away, "And give me one."

Again, you really make the choice depending on what he does. You have to do it quickly and smoothly.

If he gives you the right ball, hold it up proudly. Grin. Have the other two balls opened and read. Then give him the one you are holding to read.

If he gives you the wrong ball, tell him to hold on to his tightly. Don't let anyone touch it until the other two are read.

But if he picks up two wrong balls, look pleased and ask him to read the message on each of them. Then he is to read the message on the ball he decided to leave!

You see, you just can't lose because you don't tell him ahead of time whether he is choosing balls to keep or balls not to keep. It is important to look happy every time he makes a choice, and to go on smoothly and quickly with the next step.

Don't ever repeat this trick, of course. That is even more important with this trick than some of the others. Once is enough.

TRICKS WITH DIFFERENT THINGS

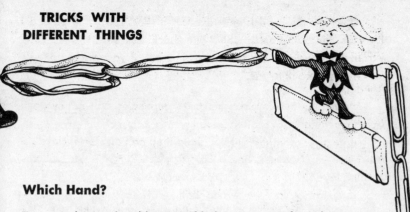

Which Hand?

Everyone knows the old game of hiding a piece of candy or gum in one hand behind your back, and then making a friend guess which hand holds the prize.

Here is a magical way to make your friend guess wrong as often as you want!

A stick of gum is the best thing to use. Open a fresh pack for the trick. This makes it seem, without your saying anything, that you have to open the pack to get a piece of gum. And this makes it seem that you use only one piece. Never say you use only one piece, however. Don't do anything to raise the idea that there might be another piece.

Because that is the secret of the trick. You have another hidden piece of gum just like the one you get from the pack. You have it stuck under your belt in the back. Wear a jacket or a sweater for this trick, so nobody sees the extra gum sticking out of your belt.

Cast a Spell

"Do you believe in hoodoo?" you ask. "Suppose I can throw a magic spell over you so you cannot pick the hand that holds the gum?"

Open the fresh pack and take out a stick. Leave the pack on the table. Put both hands behind your back. Pull out the extra stick with the empty hand. Hold both fists in front of you, backs up. Ask your friend to point to one.

WHICH HAND HAS
THE STICK OF GUM?

"Wrong," you say, opening the *other* fist to show the gum. "It's over here."

Put both hands behind your back again. Shuffle them a bit, as if changing the gum from hand to hand. Hold them out in front again. Whichever hand your friend chooses, open the other one to show she is wrong.

Five or six tries is about enough. On the final try, put one piece of gum behind your belt and bring out one hand with gum and one hand empty.

If she chooses the wrong hand again, you can end on a miracle. Show the empty hand and the gum in the other hand. "That's enough for now," you say.

If she chooses the hand with the gum, grin happily. "I knew you could break the spell sooner or later," you say. "Here's your reward."

Give her the gum whether she choses right or wrong, for being such a good sport.

After each choice, put your hands behind your back right away, but without seeming to be in too much of a hurry. If you hesitate, she may ask to see both hands. The way to stop this is to get your hands behind your back before she can ask.

The Jumping
Rubber Band

With two rubber bands, you can do a simple little trick that will have your friends wondering for a long time.

Start by finding two rubber bands that are a fairly tight fit around the base of all your fingers except the thumb. The size is not very important, but it will be easiest if the band fits snugly around your fingers. You can double a band that is too long.

Put one of the bands around the first two fingers of your left hand, as in the picture. "Watch," you say. "Matter through matter!"

Holding your hand palm up, pull the band up from the *palm* side with all the fingers of your right hand to spread it wide. Now curl your left fingers into your palm under the rubber band and let it down across your knuckles. See the pictures to make this clear.

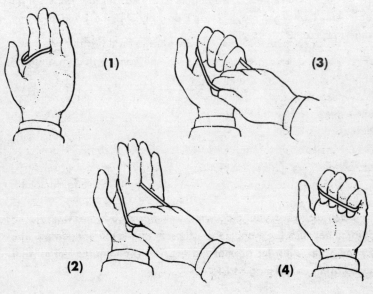

(1)

(2)

(3)

(4)

You are ready to do the first part of the trick. Hold your hand out. Make mysterious passes with your right hand. Straighten the left fingers quickly. Magically, the band jumps from the first two fingers to the last two fingers!

It Jumps Back

Pull the band up with your right hand again, curl your left fingers under it, and let the band snap down across all the knuckles of your left hand. Straighten them. The band jumps back to the first two fingers.

"Some people think I slip the band over the tips of my fingers," you say. "Let me prove that it really does go through my fingers."

With the first rubber band still around the base of the first two fingers, weave the other band around the tips of your left fingers. Crisscross it between each two fingers so it holds all four fingers tight together. "Now," you say, "I can't possibly slip the band over my fingertips, can I?"

Do just what you did before. It works just the way it did before, because the band really flips over *all* your fingertips. The second band is just for dramatic effect. This is one of the easiest and most baffling of all magic tricks!

The Linking
Paper Clips

You show a dollar bill or strong piece of paper about the same size.
You show two paper clips. Folding the bill, you slip the paper clips
over it separately. Jerk the ends of the bill. The paper clips pop
off—*linked together!*

Now you let your friend try. Fold up the bill and put the paper
clips on. He jerks the ends. The paper clips fly off—but they do not
link. You can do it again and let him fail again. It's baffling.

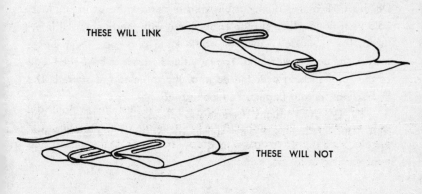

THESE WILL LINK

THESE WILL NOT

The secret is the way you put the clips on. You fold the bill in thirds, like the picture. The clips go over only two layers of paper. When you want them to link, put each clip over two layers near the *ends* of the bills. When you want them not to link, put them over two layers near the *folds* in the bill. The difference is hard to notice, but it makes them link or not link.

Try this out by yourself. Try it both ways until you get a feel for how to put the clips on without having to think. Near the ends to link. Near the folds not to link.

The Magnetized Knife

Do this trick at the dinner table with a clean knife at your place. Fold your hands, then straighten them out with the fingers still interlaced. Lay them down over the table knife and raise them, backs toward the people watching. You may find it easier to have the blade of the knife sticking over the edge of the table to get started. The knife clings to your fingers. You look proud.

But everyone laughs because your thumbs are hidden. So you raise your left thumb. People still laugh. Raise your right thumb—after you have put your left thumb back.

Everyone is sure you are just using your thumbs. So you fool them all by raising both thumbs. The knife still clings to your fingers!

The secret is simple. When you fold your hands, put the second finger of the right hand *inside* instead of through the other fingers. There are only seven fingers and two thumbs showing on the other side, but nobody ever notices this. Besides, your little act with the thumbs takes their attention away from your fingers.

You hold the knife between this extra finger and the base of your left fingers. That's all there is to it!

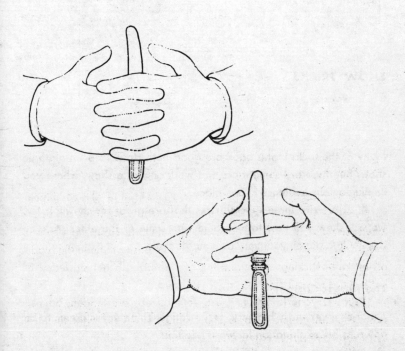

SHOW TRICKS

Many of the tricks in this book are good both close up or in a magic show. But there are some tricks that work only in a show, where you can keep your audience in one place.

Here are three special tricks that are great for shows. Later, we will show you how to mix them with some of the other tricks in this book to put on your very own magic show.

The Magic Clipper

This trick is very easy but very, very strange. There doesn't seem to be any possible explanation for what happens.

What you seem to do, during the show, is cut a strip of paper from a newspaper. Hold it up for everyone to see. Now fold the

[56]

strip in the middle. Hold it up high with the fold down, the ends between your thumb and fingers as in the picture. Taking the scissors, you cut the fold off.

Smile. Let the end toward you—the one between your thumb and first finger—drop.

The cut has healed itself! The paper is in one piece again, even though everyone saw you cut the fold off.

Fold it again and take another cut. Drop the end toward you. Again—the cut disappears! The paper seems whole again—even though the cut-off fold is on the floor.

Again and again you cut and heal, cut and heal, until finally you have just a scrap of paper left. Smile at everyone as you show it around, drop it with all the cut-off folds on the floor, and then sweep them all up and put them in your pocket.

It's good to be neat, of course, But, more important, you don't want anyone looking at the scraps.

How It Works

The secret is very simple. You prepare the newspaper in a special way that makes the trick work itself!

You need some rubber cement. No other kind will work, so make sure the tube or bottle *says* rubber cement. And you need some plain talcum powder. Baby powder works fine.

Smear a coat of rubber cement on the strip of paper you will later cut out of the newspaper. Cover the strip thoroughly. Smooth out the cement while it is still wet. There should not be a *thick* layer of cement. Now go away and let it dry. Let it dry for several hours or even overnight.

When the cement is completely dry, cover it with talcum powder. Make sure to cover it all. Rub the powder around lightly to make sure. Then shake the loose powder off.

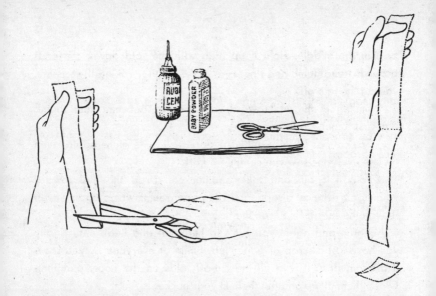

From a little distance, the paper looks ordinary. If it doesn't, you used too much cement. The paper should be covered thoroughly but not thickly. A little practice will teach you how much to use.

When it is time for the trick, pick up the newspaper. Cut out the part you have prepared with rubber cement and powder. Wave it around so everyone can see it.

Fold the paper with the cement *inside*. This is important. The talcum powder will keep the cement from sticking until the scissors cut and squeeze through the powder. Hold one end between your first and second fingers, the other between thumb and first finger. The folded end hangs down. Cut off the fold about an inch from the bottom so everyone can see that you really cut it. The cut will go through the talcum powder and the scissors will squeeze the rubber cement together. Pause for just a moment. Then let the end toward you drop. Pause again to let everyone gasp.

The effect is very eerie. You'll like it.

The Rope
through the Girl

Many magicians with big stage shows feature a trick called "sawing a girl in half." This needs a lot of expensive equipment.

You can do something very much like it with nothing but a piece of rope.

Get hold of an old piece of clothesline, or a long jump rope, about eight to twelve feet long. It should be well used so it is very soft and flexible.

The trick is really all in your acting and one very simple "move." Practice the move with a trusted friend many times until you can do it quickly and easily, without fumbling—or just practice on yourself.

The only thing you have to look out for is that when you do the trick, you pick a girl—or boy—who is wearing a belt.

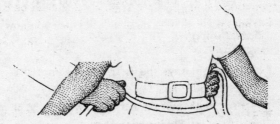

What You
Seem to Do

Toss one end of the rope out to a strong-looking boy in the audience. "Please examine it," you say. "I've been accused of using a trick rope for this next trick."

Pull on your end of the rope. Try to get a little comedy in your tug of war. "You can't find the trick?" you go on. "Good. Then would you please come up and help me?"

Now look around for a girl who is wearing a belt. You might

have one already set beforehand, if you want. The girl might or might not catch on to the trick. It is a good idea to talk to her first and get her to promise to keep the secret. Even then, she may not figure it out.

Have her come up and stand farther back than the boy is. "You wait there until we're ready," you tell him.

Take the rope in both hands. Stand behind the girl. Reaching up with your hands about two feet apart, pass the rope over the girl's head. Bring it down to her waist. You have one hand on each side.

"Raise your arms, please," you tell her. "Now," you say, "around, across in back, and tie in front."

You do all this. Call your helper over now. "You take this end," you tell him. "I'll take this one."

You both back away. The girl stands there with the rope around her, tied in front.

"We'll try not to hurt you. Are you scared?" you ask.

Right through the Girl

After the girl says she is scared, or that she is not, call to your helper. "Ready? Pull!"

You both pull on the rope. Magically, it melts right through the girl's waist. *But the knot stays!*

Your helper can examine the rope again, and the knot, as much as he wants. There is nothing wrong.

How It Works

There is nothing to get ready ahead of time, except perhaps to make arrangements with the girl. You really do the trick when you seem to cross the rope behind her back.

Instead of crossing it, you just jam a loop from each side under her belt. Then you bring each end out the *same* way it came back. One simple overhand knot in front, and you are ready.

When you pretend to cross the rope, make sure to bring both ends all the way behind the girl for a moment so your audience loses track of which end is which. And make very sure you do it right, or you will squeeze her when you pull on the rope.

Practice this until you can do it quickly and easily. And always *say* "across in back" loudly as you tuck the rope into her belt.

Imagine such a feature trick with one piece of rope!

Candy from Nowhere

A good way to start any magic show is with a surprise trick. And there are few better surprises than a magical appearance.

Instead of fancy boxes or tubes, or even scarves, this trick uses a sheet of newspaper. From it, you produce a box of candy or Cracker Jacks!

Here is how you get ready.

Take a box of Cracker Jacks, or a *light* box of candy about the same size. Make sure it does not have a cellophane wrapper so it won't rustle while you are keeping it secret. With a large needle, pull a piece of black thread through one end and out the side, as in the picture. Tie a knot so the box hangs from the thread. Use the lightest thread you can that you are sure will not break, and make sure to test it before you show the trick.

Now tie a large loop in the other end of the thread. Make the

loop big enough so that you can get your left thumb in and out of it easily. The thread from box to loop should be just long enough so that it is not quite tight when the box is held under the *right* armpit, under your jacket, and your left hand is held out in front of you to read a newspaper.

Try out everything, including the way you produce the box, in front of a mirror. Do it many times before you show the trick.

How It Works

Begin your show by walking out reading a newspaper. Hold it in front of you to hide the thread going from right armpit to left thumb as you read the headlines.

Look over the top of the newspaper at your audience. "What do you do with a newspaper?" you say. "Well, this is what a magician might do with a used newspaper."

Holding one corner of the newspaper in your left hand, take away all but one sheet with your right. Toss the extra newspaper to one side. Hold up the one sheet between you and the audience.

"Nothing on your side of the paper," you say, showing it.

Bring your left hand over behind your right hand to show the other side of the paper. The thread will still be hidden. "Nothing on the other side either, except news."

Bring the sheet back the way it was. Raise your left hand so that the paper hangs down at an angle in front of you, and curl it a little with the middle toward the audience. Move your right hand to the bottom to help straighten and then curl the paper. Raise your left hand high enough to tighten the thread.

Start to put your right hand behind the paper. Then look up suddenly. "No, there's nothing in my hand," you say. Raise it high and *look at it*. Show it front and back.

Everybody looks at your hand, just as the box swings down behind the newspaper! "But with magic," you say, "we can get some good news from this newspaper."

Tear the Newspaper

With your right hand—which you just showed empty—reach behind the newspaper and grab the box. With your left hand, crumple the newspaper around it to show the shape of the box. Tear the crumpled newspaper away from the top. Try to snap the thread and carry it away with the newspaper. Hold up the box. "This looks like good news!" you say.

Open the box, tearing the thread away with the end if you did not get rid of it with the newspaper. Offer the candy around if you like.

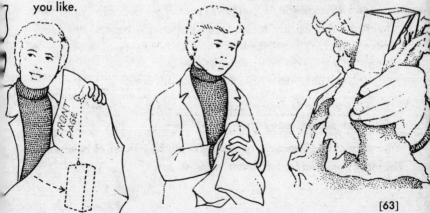

YOUR OWN MAGIC SHOW

Here is a whole magic show put together from the tricks in this book.

You can use other tricks, or add tricks you learn or buy somewhere else. But try to keep each trick different. One magical appearance, one magical disappearance, one magical repair, and so on.

Go over your plan carefully. Make sure to remember which trick comes next. Make sure you have everything you need, and have the things where you can get each one quickly when it is needed for a trick.

A corner or a doorway makes a good "stage." It keeps people from seeing around the sides. Set up chairs for your audience, or have them sit on the floor.

Be extra careful if you give your show for young children. They are much harder to fool than grown-ups, because they look where you don't want them to look and may even come up on "stage" to handle the things you have ready.

This is a good show from the tricks in this book:

Candy from Nowhere. You have to use this trick first, because of the way you get ready for it.

The Magic Clipper. You can have another sheet of newspaper already prepared for this. Don't forget scissors!

The Knot That Ties Itself with a handkerchief. Be sure you have the knot ready!

The Knot That Melts Away with the same handkerchief.

The Vanishing Handkerchief. This gets rid of the handkerchief for you. You have to wear a jacket, anyway, to show *Candy from Nowhere*. Don't forget to have your "pull" ready. You can get it from your hip pocket while you are asking someone to examine the handkerchief for signs of the knot you made disappear.

With a deck of cards, you can now do:

Behind Your Back. The reversed card will surprise everyone. When you go through the cards looking for one you could not find, show everyone in the audience rather than just the person you called on "stage" to help you.

The Rope through the Girl is a feature trick.

The Three Choices is a good trick to end with. You can tear up pieces of newspaper for this. Make sure to have a pencil for the messages.

This makes eight magic tricks. That is about right for a magic show like this. Every one is a baffler!

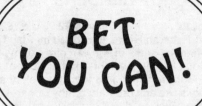

WORLDS OF WONDER
FROM
AVON CAMELOT

THE INDIAN IN THE CUPBOARD
60012-9/$2.95US/$3.95Can
THE RETURN OF THE INDIAN
70284-3/$2.95US only

Lynne Reid Banks

"Banks conjures up a story that is both thoughtful and captivating and interweaves the fantasy with care and believability" *Booklist*

THE HUNKY-DORY DAIRY
Anne Lindbergh 70320-3/$2.75US/$3.75Can

"A beguiling fantasy...full of warmth, wit and charm"
Kirkus Reviews

THE MAGIC OF THE GLITS
C.S. Adler 70403-X/$2.50US/$3.50Can

"A truly magical book" *The Reading Teacher*

GOOD-BYE PINK PIG
C.S. Adler 70175-8/$2.75US/$3.25 Can

Every fifth grader needs a friend she can count on!

BOOK FOUR

Sir Arthur Conan Doyle's
THE ADVENTURES OF
SHERLOCK HOLMES

Adapted for young readers by Catherine Edwards Sadler

The Adventure of the Reigate Puzzle Holmes comes near death to unravel a devilish case of murder and blackmail.

The Adventure of the Crooked Man The key to this strange mystery lies in the deadly secrets of a wicked man's past.

The Adventure of the Greek Interpreter Sherlock's brilliant older brother joins Holmes on the hunt for a bunch of ruthless villains in a case of kidnapping.

The Adventure of the Naval Treaty Only Holmes can untangle a case that threatens the national security of England, and becomes a matter of life and death.

Join the uncanny and extraordinary Sherlock Holmes, and his friend and chronicler Dr. Watson, as they tackle dangerous crimes and untangle the most intricate mysteries.

AVON CAMELOT

Sherlock 4-4/88